W9-CQP-113

2

FIRST GRADERS from MARS

Episode 4: Tera, Star Student

Story by **SHANA COREY**

Pictures by **MARK TEAGUE**

SCHOLASTIC PRESS · NEW YORK

Text copyright © 2003 by Shana Corey
Illustrations copyright © 2003 by Mark Teague
All rights reserved. Published by Scholastic Press, a division of Scholastic Inc.,
Publishers since 1920. SCHOLASTIC and SCHOLASTIC PRESS and associated logos are
trademarks and/or registered trademarks of Scholastic Inc.

No part of this publication may be reproduced, or stored in a retrieval system, or transmitted in any form or
by any means, electronic, mechanical, photocopying, recording, or otherwise, without written permission
of the publisher. For information regarding permission, write to Scholastic Inc., Attention:
Permissions Department, 557 Broadway, New York, NY 10012.
Library of Congress Cataloging-in-Publication Data:
Corey, Shana.
First graders from Mars. Episode 4, Tera, star student / story by Shana Corey;
pictures by Mark Teague. p. cm. Summary: Although she is smart, Tera must learn
the importance of working together on a group project.
ISBN 0-439-26634-3
[1. Behavior—Fiction. 2. Extraterrestrial beings—Fiction. 3. Schools—Fiction. 4. Mars (Planet)—Fiction.]
I. Title: Tera, star student. II. Teague, Mark, ill. III. Title. PZ7.C8155 Fn 2003 [E]--dc21 2002009569
10 9 8 7 6 5 4 3 2 1   03 04 05 06 07
Printed in Mexico   49
First edition, July 2003
The text type was set in 18-point Martin Gothic Medium.
Book design by Kristina Albertson

For my mom

— SC

To Emily: Have a happy first grade!

— MT

Tera was a star student.

When Pod 1 practiced letters,

Tera wrote a 300-page book.

When Pod 1 carried numbers,
Tera carried hers farther than anyone.
It was hard work being a star,
but it was worth it.

"Meep, meep,"
said Ms. Vortex one morning.
"Today we will do group projects.
Each group will make a model of a planet.
I know we will all work together."

Horus, Pelly, Nergal, and Tera
were in Group Earth.
They cut. They colored.
They patted. They pasted.
"Don't worry," promised Tera.
"I will make sure we get gold stars."

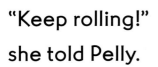

"Keep rolling!"
she told Pelly.

"More blue!"
she told Horus.

"Nobo!" she cried when
Nergal drew an earthling.
"Everyone knows
earthlings are not real."

She tossed the earthling into the trash.

"Heybey!" said Nergal.

"What about our ideas?"

"You think you are so smart," said Pelly.

"You are not the boss of us," said Horus.

"I am smart," said Tera.

"And I am not being bossy,

I am being right."

Tera grabbed the model and pulled.
Pelly, Horus, and Nergal pulled back.
Splat!
"NOW LOOK WHAT YOU'VE DONE!"
yelled Tera.

Tera spent the rest of the hour in time-out.
She watched Group Saturn
make rings together.
She watched Group Earth
make a moon together.

"Laba! Laba! Laba!" she sang to herself.

"I do not need Group Earth."

She peeked over to see if they heard her.

They were too busy working together to notice.

At recess,
Tera played alone.
She played tag,
but no one chased her.

She played movie star,
but no one clapped.

She played hide-and-seek,
but no one looked for her.

Finally, she sat
and watched Pelly, Horus, and Nergal
play supermartians together.
"Laba. Laba. Laba," she warbled.
It was not a very fun recess.

At the end of the day,
Ms. Vortex gave out gold stars.
"You forgot MY star," said Tera.

"I am sorry Tera," said Ms. Vortex.
"You did not work
with your group today."
"Nobo fair!" said Tera.

Tera stomped home.

When she got there,

she threw her backpack on the floor.

"What's wrong, moonbeam?" asked Tera's dad.

"Everything," said Tera.
"I did not get a gold star.
Group Earth ruined my project.
And Ms. Vortex blamed me."
She clomped into her room.

She ripped her gold stars off the wall.

She tore her pod picture into pieces.

Tera's dad knocked on the door.

"Do you want to talk?" he asked.

"Nobo," said Tera. "I want to change pods."

"But your friends are in Pod 1," said Tera's dad.

"Not anymore," said Tera.
"You can't change pods every time
something goes wrong," said Tera's dad.
"That's not like my moonbeam."

That night,
Tera's family read together.
Tera picked out a book
about her favorite supermartians,
the Alien All-Stars.

In the story, an evil earthling
captured Captain Comet.
The Alien All-Stars flew in to save her.
"'That will teach you!' said Captain Comet.
'When the Alien All-Stars work together,
nothing can stop us!'
The end," read Tera.

After the story,

Tera's parents tucked her into bed.

Tera snuggled under her covers.

But she could not fall asleep.

She thought about Group Earth.

She thought about the Alien All-Stars.

Finally, she climbed out of bed.

She picked up the pieces of her pod picture.

Then she taped them back together.

The next day at school,

Tera found Group Earth.

"Good news!" she said.

"I will be part of the group again."

Horus, Pelly, and Nergal looked at each other.

Tera took a deep breath.

"And I am sorry I was bossy," she said.

"I will work together now.

Will you forgive me?"

Horus, Pelly, and Nergal smiled.

"Yebes," said Pelly.

"You may be bossy," said Horus.

"But you are still our friend."

"And you do have good ideas," said Nergal.

"That's true!" agreed Tera.

Group Earth went to work.
Together they made
oceans and rivers, lakes and land.
"Let's make clouds," said Nergal.
"Well . . ." started Tera.
Everyone looked at her.
"Great idea!" she said.

At the end of the day,
each group held up their planet.
When they let go,
the planets floated around the pod.
"Wobow," said Tera.
"Together we made a whole solar system!"

Ms. Vortex gave everyone gold stars.

"Great job, Martians!" she said.

"We know!" said Tera.

She gave her friends a high five.

"We are an all-star group!"